DIARY OF A WORM

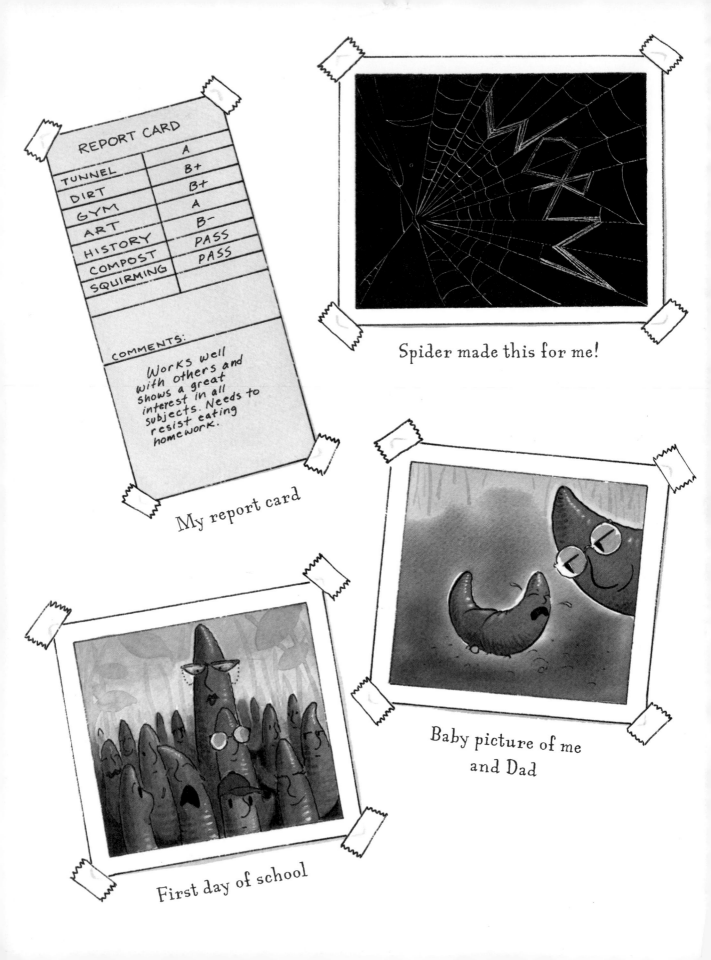

REPORT CARD

	A
TUNNEL	B+
DIRT	B+
GYM	A
ART	B-
HISTORY	PASS
COMPOST	PASS
SQUIRMING	

COMMENTS:

Works well with others and shows a great interest in all subjects. Needs to resist eating homework.

My report card

Spider made this for me!

Baby picture of me and Dad

First day of school

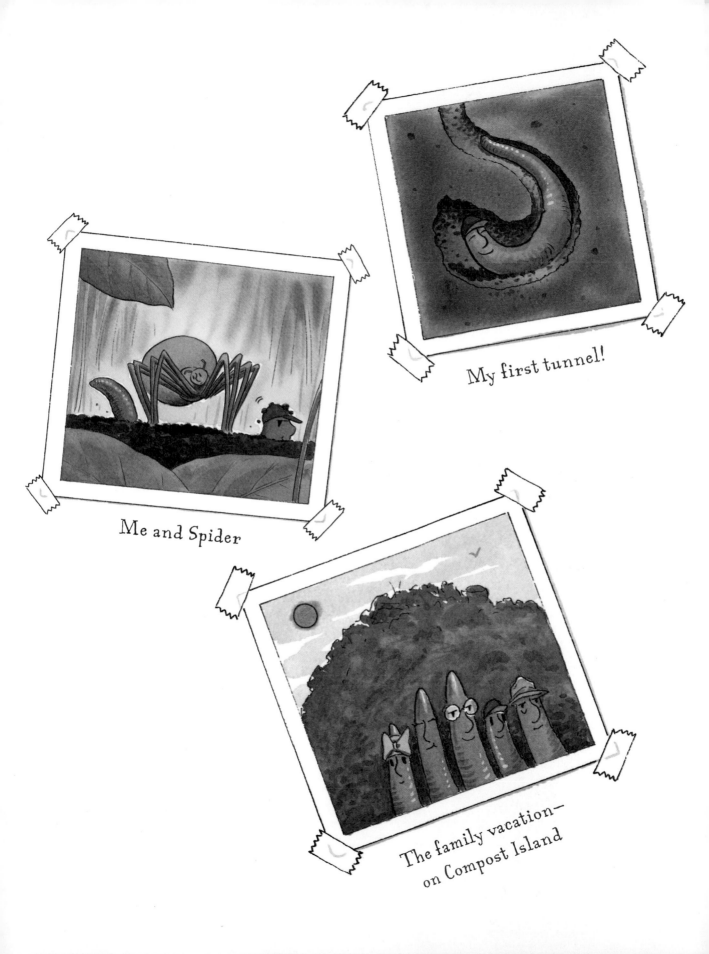

My first tunnel!

Me and Spider

The family vacation—
on Compost Island

For "the boys"—
Ken, Sean, Ryan, Patrick and Timothy
—D.C.

For Rozzie and Cheetah
—H.B.

ISBN 0-439-69234-2

Text copyright © 2003 by Doreen Cronin. Illustrations copyright © 2003 by Harry Bliss. All rights reserved. Published by Scholastic Inc., 557 Broadway, New York, NY 10012, by arrangement with HarperCollins Publishers. SCHOLASTIC and associated logos are trademarks and/or registered trademarks of Scholastic Inc.

12 11 10 9 8 7 6 5 4 3 2 1   4 5 6 7 8 9/0
Printed in the U.S.A.   40
First Scholastic printing, September 2004
Typography by Alicia Mikles.

DIARY OF A WORM

By Doreen Cronin
Pictures by Harry Bliss

SCHOLASTIC INC.
New York Toronto London Auckland Sydney
Mexico City New Delhi Hong Kong Buenos Aires

MARCH 20

Mom says there are three things
I should always remember:

1. The earth gives us everything
we need.

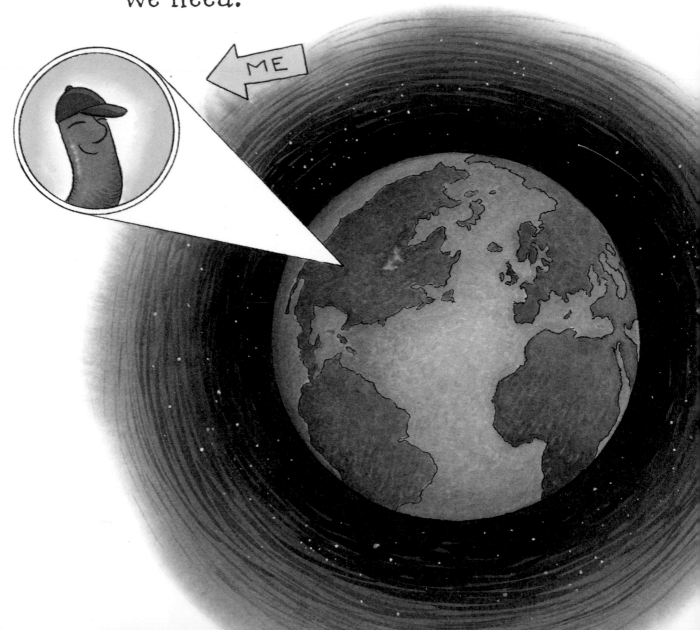

2. When we dig tunnels, we help take care of the earth.

3. Never bother Daddy when he's eating the newspaper.

First all of his legs got stuck.

Then he swallowed a bunch of dirt.

Tomorrow he's going to teach
me how to walk upside down.

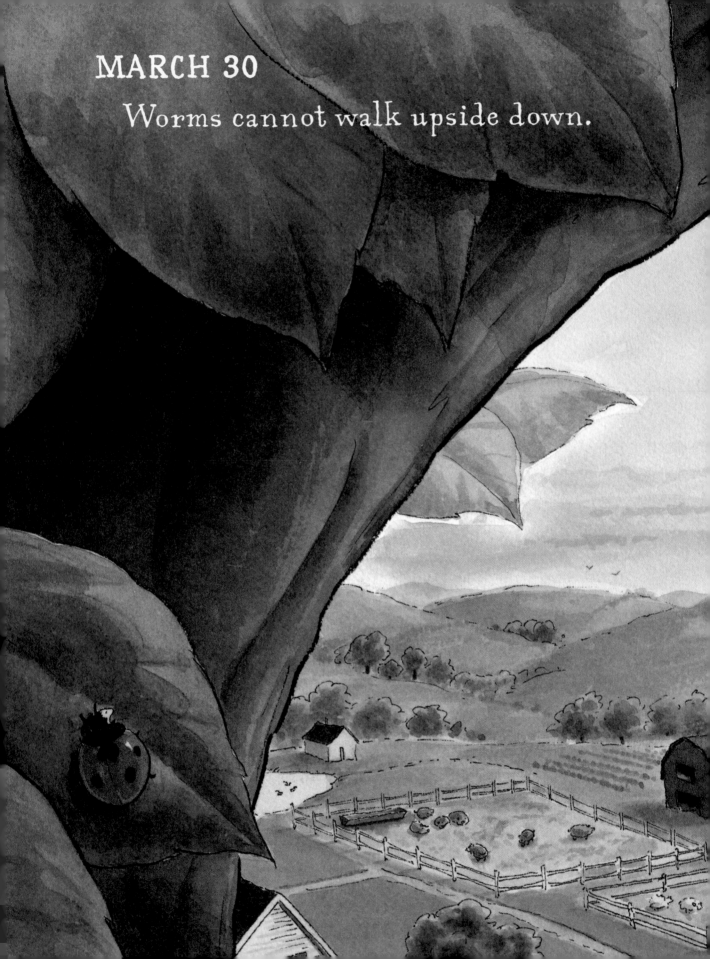

MARCH 30

Worms cannot walk upside down.

APRIL 4

Fishing season started today.
We all dug deeper.

APRIL 10

It rained all night and the ground was soaked. We spent the entire day on the sidewalk.

Hopscotch is a very dangerous game.

APRIL 15

I forgot my lunch today.
I got so hungry that I ate
my homework.

My teacher made me write "I will not eat my homework" ten times.

When I was finished, I ate that, too.

APRIL 20

I snuck up on some kids in the park today. They didn't hear me coming.

I wiggled up right between them and they SCREAMED.

I love when they do that.

Grandpa taught us that good
manners are very important.

So today I said "good morning"
to the first ant I saw.

MAY 8

Had the worst nightmare
last night—

giant birds playing hopscotch.

Mom says I have to stop eating so much garbage right before I go to bed.

MAY 15

I got into a fight with Spider today.
He told me you need legs to be cool.
Then he ran. I couldn't keep up.
Maybe he's right.

MAY 16

I made Spider laugh so hard,
he fell out of his tree.
Who needs legs?

MAY 28

Last night I went to the school dance.

You put your head in.

You put your head out.

You do the hokey pokey and
you turn yourself about.

That's all we could do.

I brought mine home and
we ate it for dinner.

JUNE 15

My older sister thinks she's so pretty. I told her that no matter how much time she spends looking in the mirror, her face will always look just like her rear end.

Spider thought that
was really funny.

Mom did not.

When I grow up, I want to be a Secret Service agent. Spider says I will have to be very careful because the president might step on me by mistake.

JULY 28

Three things I don't like about being a worm:

1. I can't chew gum.

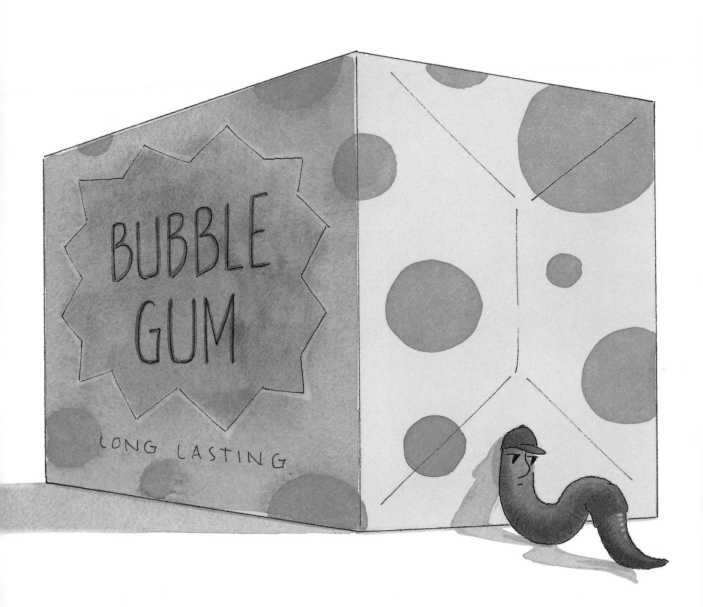

2. I can't have a dog.

3. All that homework.

Three good things about being a worm:

1. I never have to go to the dentist.

2. I never get in trouble for tracking mud through the house.

3. I never have to take a bath.

AUGUST 1

It's not always easy being a worm. We're very small, and sometimes people forget that we're even here.

But, like Mom always says, the earth never forgets we're here.

KITCHEN

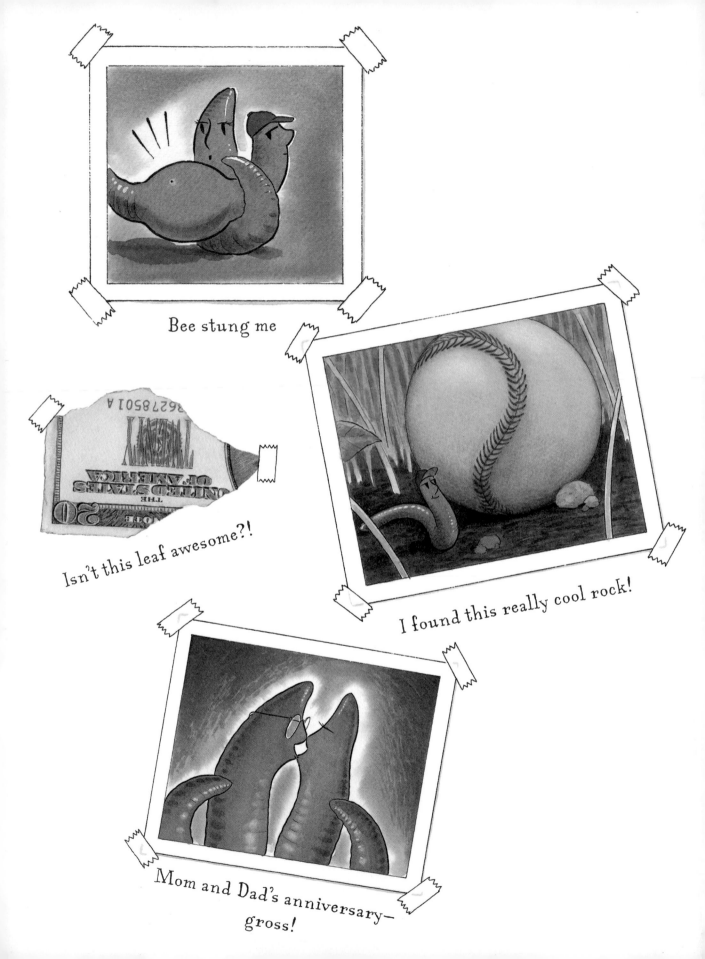

Bee stung me

Isn't this leaf awesome?!

I found this really cool rock!

Mom and Dad's anniversary—
gross!